For the child in everyone

THIS BOOK BELONGS TO

children's choice®

American text copyright © 1981 Scholastic Inc.
ISBN: 0-590-75822-5
Printed in U.S.A.

IF DINOSAURS WERE CATS AND DOGS

COLIN McNAUGHTON

Adapted by Alice Low

A Children's Choice® Book Club Edition From Scholastic Book Services

Ernest Benn
LONDON & TONBRIDGE

"Goodbye, dear cat, I'm going away.
I'm flying off to distant shores,
Where tiny snails are big as whales
And cats are big as dinosaurs."

The molehills in this crazy land
Are mountains where folks play and climb,
But when a mole breaks through its hole
It spoils a picnic every time.

This land is full of oddities,
You never know quite what you'll find.
This hunter sees a tower of cheese,
But will he see what lurks behind?

Most people paddle, dive or swim
In lakes or pools or swimming holes,
But here they play and spend the day
Inside a giant goldfish bowl.

This cat looks most contented now.
It's had a hundred tons of food,
But it can snap and scare a chap
When it is in a hungry mood.

They work all day so they can pay
To feed their hound its daily feast,
But when they're done, they think it's fun
To ride upon their giant beast.

"I much prefer to fly a frog.
This is the life!" the pilot cries.
"With one great bound I leave the ground
And play at leapfrog in the skies."

The farmers need a net to catch
These giant eggs. It's quite a sight!
Such long, long legs mean scrambled eggs
When hens lay eggs from such a height.

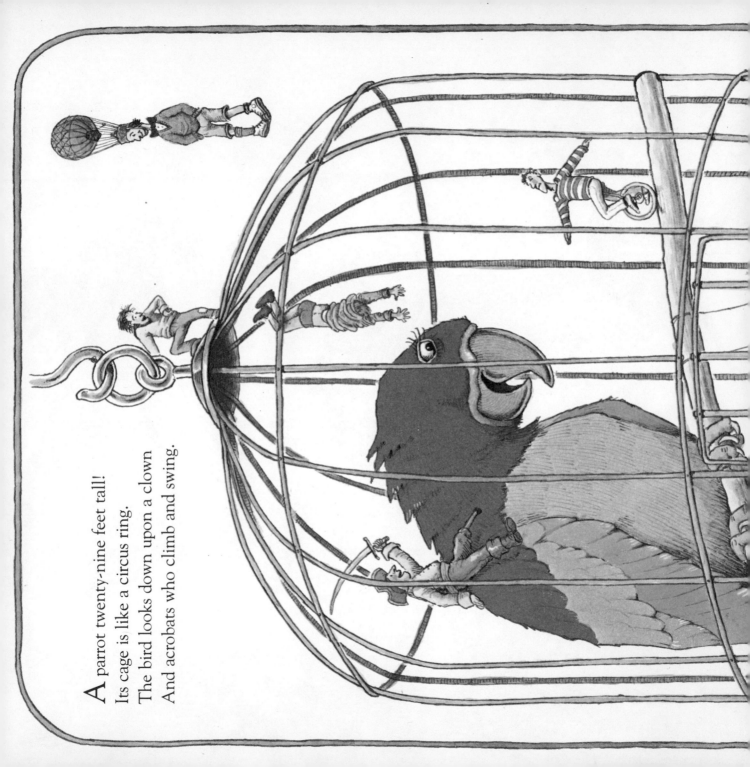

A parrot twenty-nine feet tall!
Its cage is like a circus ring.
The bird looks down upon a clown
And acrobats who climb and swing.

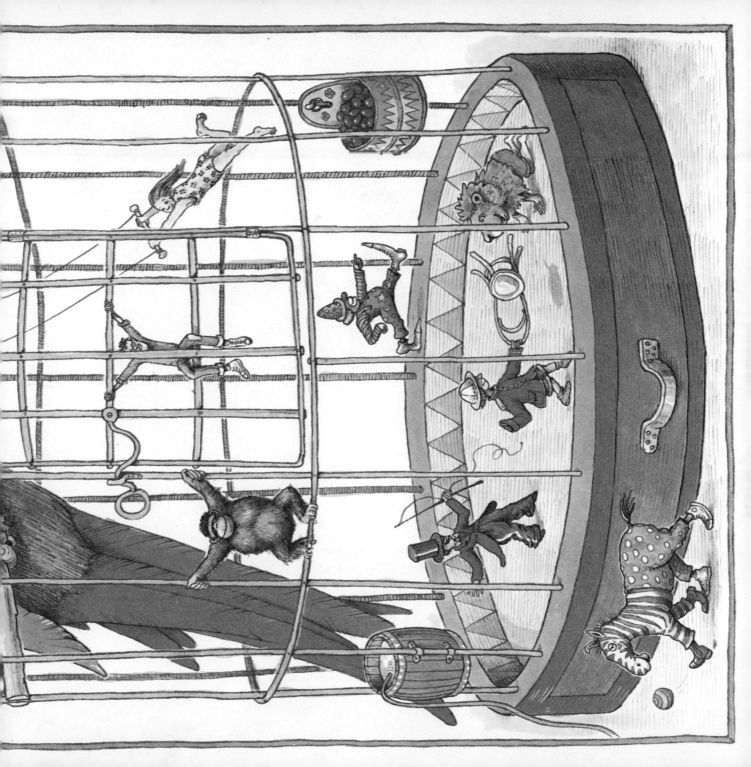

Awakened from a long, deep sleep,
The tortoise lifts its weary head.
The dark brown shell it knew so well
Is used for winter sports instead!

The engineers who run this train
    Look back and can't believe their eyes.
        A passenger with spines and fur
            Has jumped on board. What a surprise!

This snake is over ten miles long,
Which makes it very hard to steer.
When people shout, "Look out! Look out!"
Its head's too far away to hear.

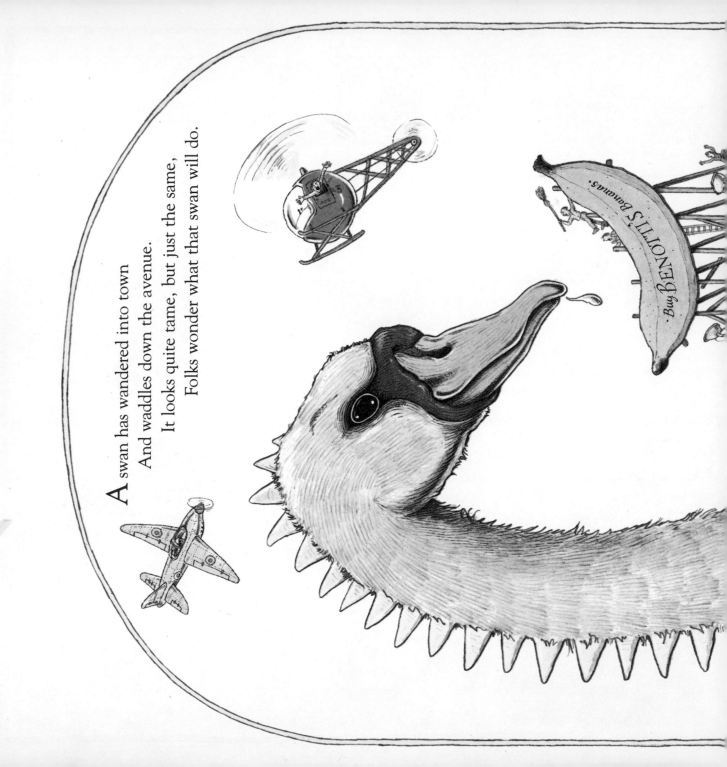

A swan has wandered into town
And waddles down the avenue.
It looks quite tame, but just the same,
Folks wonder what that swan will do.

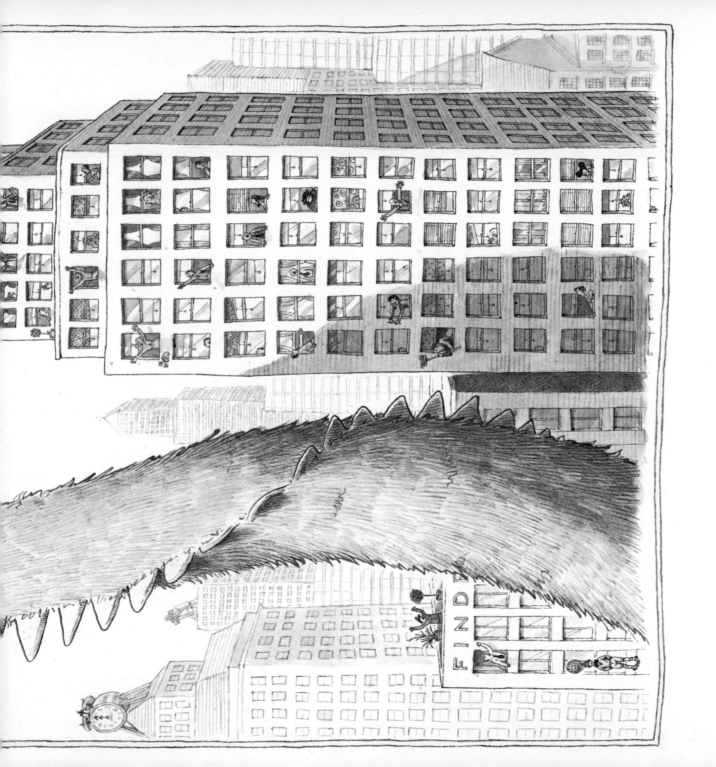

A frightened butcher speeds away.
The pig is giving chase. Says he,
"I'll catch that man inside that van.
He won't make sausage meat of me!"

MISTER BONES
THE
BUTCHER

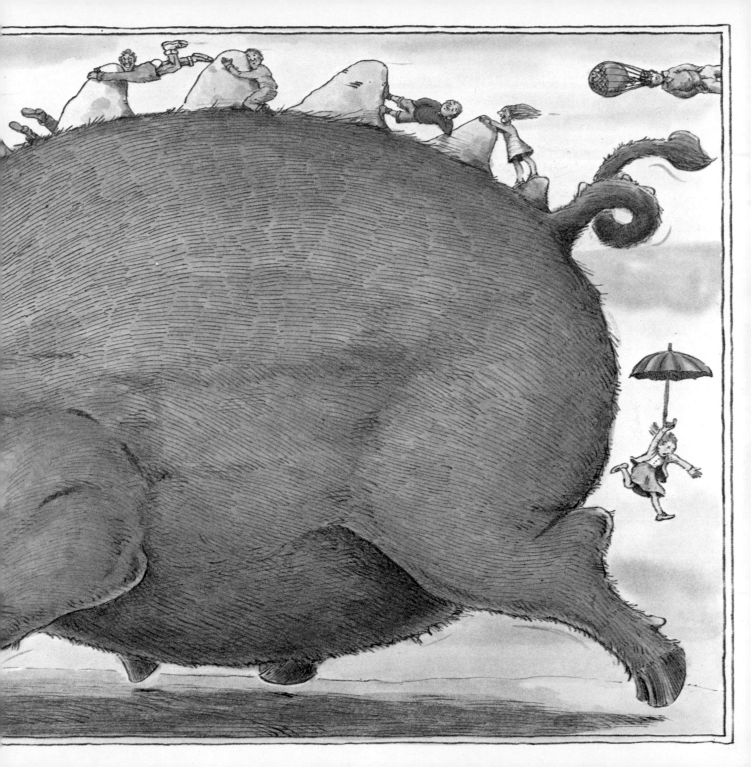

A giant hedgehog runs through town
And leads folks on a merry chase.
A washing line's stuck to its spines.
I wonder who will win the race?

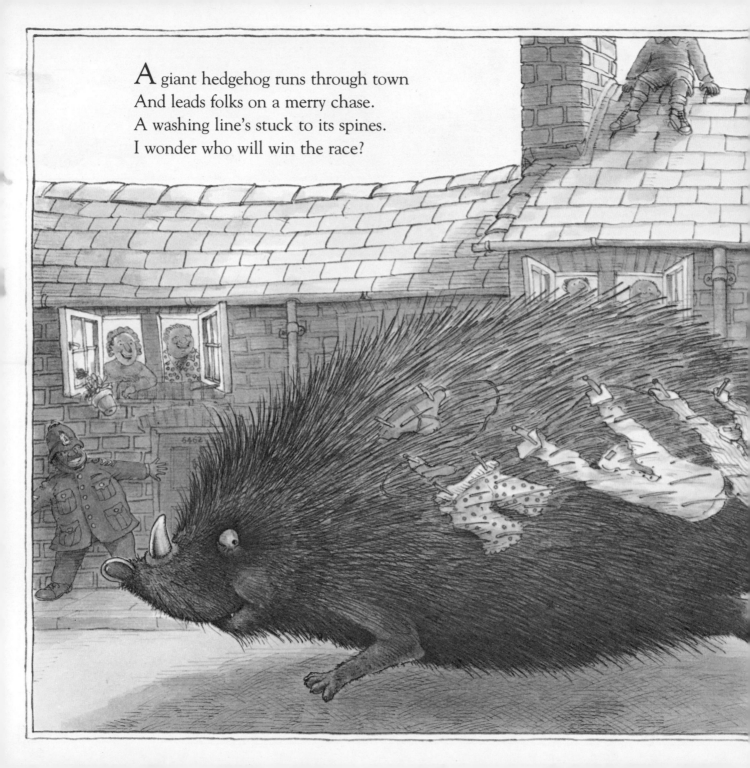

"Hello, dear cat, I'm home again,
And very glad to be here, too,
Where frogs are frogs and dogs are dogs,
And cats are small and sweet like you."

Look Who's Part of the Children's Choice® Family!

Something special for Children's Choice® Book Club members

You can get all these storybook favorites—Puss in Boots, Babar, Curious George, Lyle, George and Martha and The Year at Maple Hill Farm—to hang up on your wall. They're big (17″ × 22″) and beautiful posters, printed in full color on high quality paper. Best of all, you can get all 6 for just $3.95, including postage and handling.

To order your set of 6 Children's Choice® posters, please send your name, address and $3.95 in check or money order to:

CHILDREN'S CHOICE® POSTERS
2931 East McCarty St.
P.O. Box 1068
Jefferson City, Mo. 65102

Please allow 3-6 weeks for delivery. Your posters are mailed in a tube, so they won't be creased at all.

Offer expires December 31, 1981